The Avenger Thor throws his hammer at Loki.

Loki throws some red beams.

BANG! One hits Thor's hammer

1

Then that beam flies in front of the schoolchildren. Quickly, Kendra holds up her backpack. The beam hits it. **POP!**

"It has no powers!"

Suddenly, Kendra's backpack is very heavy.

Thor, her favorite Avenger, has a problem with his hammer.

3

Kendra goes to the lab.

"Don't put that in there, Ian!" Omar says.
Suddenly, there is a big explosion BANG!.

Kendra swings her backpack and throws it. The explosion stops! The backpack flies back to Kendra's hand.

Ms. Castro watches.

"Loki's beam hit my hammer," Thor tells Nick Fury. "Where are its powers?"

He hears Agent Castro.

Kendra sees Ian hit Omar.

"Don't hit Omar! Stop!" she says.

But Ian does not stop.

Kendra swings her backpack over her head.
Boooom!
"That's freaky!" Ian says. He runs.

"Thor does this with his hammer."

"Where's Kendra?" Thor asks.

"I don't know," Agent Castro answers.

"Loki put my hammer's powers in her backpack," Thor says.

Kendra sees two robbers. They are running.

She stops them with her backpack.

"You're good with that," a man says.

Kendra looks behind her.

"Thor!" she says,
excited.

"You're a brave girl,"
he says.

"I'm a tired girl,"
Kendra says.

"I can take your backpack to S.H.I.E.L.D. and put the powers back in my hammer," Thor says.

"Great!" Kendra says.

In the morning at school, Kendra sees her backpack and opens it.

Great job, Kendra!
Thank you,
        Nick Fury, S.H.I.E.L.D.

Activity page

Before You Read

1 **Look at the picture on page I.**
1 Are the children happy?
2 What is in Thor's hand?
3 What is Loki doing?

After You Read

2 **Match names with pictures.**

1 Kendra
2 Ms. Castro
3 Omar
4 Ian
5 Nick Fury

3 **Read. Answer the questions.**
1 Who has a hammer with powers?
2 Who has a backpack?
3 Who takes the powers from Thor's hammer and puts them in the backpack?
4 Who works for S.H.I.E.L.D.? Nick Fury or Loki?
5 Who is a teacher and works for S.H.I.E.L.D.?

Do you like this story? Try these!

Pearson Education Limited
KAO Two
KAO Park, Harlow,
Essex, CM17 9NA, England
and Associated Companies throughout the world.

ISBN: 978-1-292-20622-6
This edition first published by Pearson Education Ltd 2018
1 3 5 7 9 10 8 6 4 2

© 2018 MARVEL

The authors have asserted their moral rights in accordance
with the Copyright Designs and Patents Act 1988

Set in 19pt/23pt HeinemannRoman Bold
Printed in China
SWTC/01

Published by Pearson Education Limited

For a complete list of the titles available in the Pearson English Readers series, visit
www.pearsonenglishreaders.com.
Alternatively, write to your local Pearson Education office or
to Pearson English Readers Marketing Department,
Pearson Education, KAO Two, KAO Park, Harlow, Essex, CM17 9NA